MAMA SAURUS

For Sarah, Mamasaurus of our little Babysaurus. —S. L.

ISBN 978-1-338-10905-4

12 11 10 9 8 7 6 5 4 3 2 1   16 17 18 19 20 21

Printed in the U.S.A.   40

This edition first printing, September 2016

Design by Sara Gillingham Studio
Typeset in Block Berthold and Paperback
The illustrations in this book were rendered in brush pen and Photoshop.

MAMA SAURUS

Stephan Lomp

SCHOLASTIC INC.

Babysaurus lived in a wild jungle with his Mamasaurus.

He loved to sit high on her back
eating tender leaves. But one day . . .

. . . he slipped.

When Babysaurus dug
himself out of a pile
of leaves, he could not
see his Mamasaurus
anywhere.

But Babysaurus did see Ornito
running by.

"Hey, wait!" he called out.
"Have you seen my mama?"

"Does she run faster than the wind like my mama?" asked Ornito.

"No, she is not very fast,"
answered Babysaurus.
"But she can take huge steps."

"Sorry, I have not seen her,"
said Ornito. Then she took
off running again.

Babysaurus roamed through the
leafy jungle until he met Tritopa.

"Have you seen my mama?"
Babysaurus asked.

"Does she have a long horn
like my mama?" asked Tritopa.

"No, but she has a wonderful long neck," answered Babysaurus.

"Then, no, I haven't seen her," said Tritopa. "Sorry."

Next, Babysaurus saw Ptero
sitting high in a tree.

"Can you see my mama from up
there?" Babysaurus called out.

"Does she have wings and fly as high as the sun like my mama?" asked Ptero.

"No, she does not have wings," answered Babysaurus. "But she is taller than the tallest tree!"

"Oh!" said Ptero. "No, I don't see her." Then she flew away.

Babysaurus heard a rustle behind
a bush. It was tiny Hespero.

"Have you seen my mama?"
Babysaurus asked.

"Is she about this big like
my mama?" asked Hespero.

"No, she is much bigger than that. She's the biggest there is!" Babysaurus marveled proudly.

"That is really big!" replied Hespero.
"But I have not seen her." Then he
shrugged and bolted away.

Suddenly, Babysaurus
heard a LOUD noise.

"Could that be my mama?"
he wondered.

It certainly was not! It was Rexy.

"Excuse me, have you seen my mama?" whispered Babysaurus.

Opening just one eye, Rexy snarled, "Does she have sharp teeth like my mama?"

"No, but she grabs the yummiest leaves from the highest branches for me," replied Babysaurus.

"Leaves? Yuck! I could
never eat leaves!"
sneered Rexy. "But . . ."

Then Babysaurus
heard an even louder
noise. . . .

It was his mama.

"There you are. I was searching
all over for you!" she said, giving
Babysaurus a kiss.

"Let's find you something to eat!"

"A salad is also nice from time to time," whispered Rexy as he rushed off.

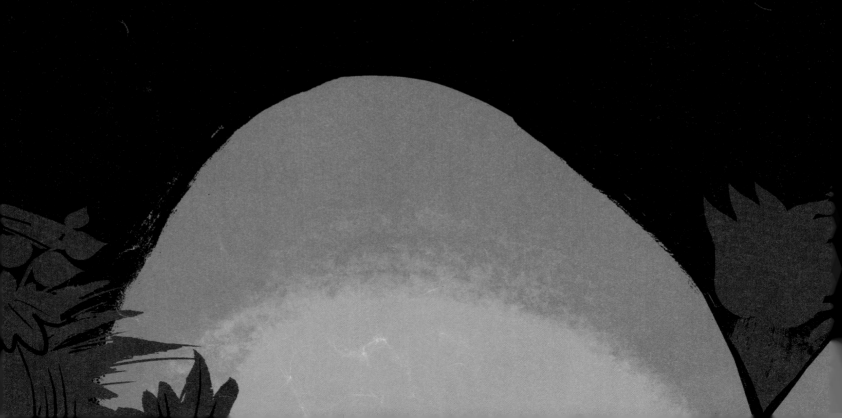

"Hooray!" cheered Babysaurus.
"You are the best Mamasaurus
in the whole jungle!"